THE THONG TREE

THE THONG TREE

Richard T. Haynes

VOYAGEUR PUBLISHING CO., INC.
Nashville, Tennessee

Printed in Singapore

Library of Congress Catalog Card Number
90-70508

Book produced by March Media, Inc., Brentwood, TN 37027
First Edition

ISBN 0-929146-02-6

*This book is lovingly dedicated to Brandon,
Ashlyn, Kendall, Hannah and to those who follow,
and most of all to Diana, who made them all possible.*

R.T.H.

C O N T E N T S

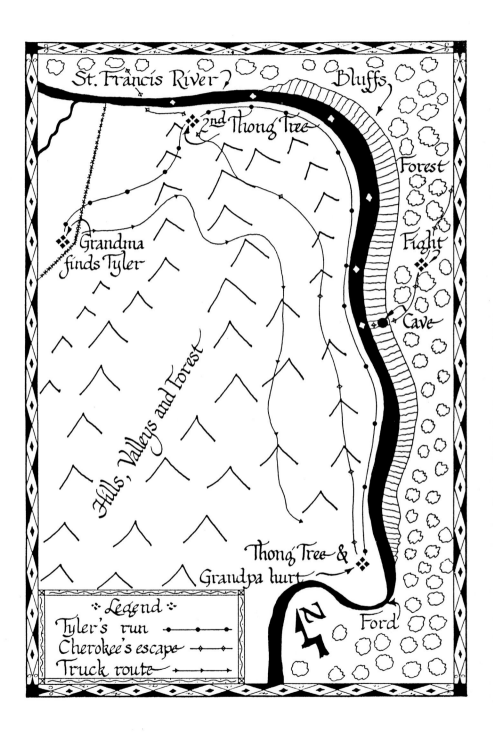

THE THONG TREE

C H A P T E R

1

Into the Woods

Tyler sprang onto a large rock at the bluff's steep edge and searched the woods below. He whistled twice, then shouted, "Rachel . . . Raaaaaa . . . chellllll! Come here, girl."

He heard only the rustle of leaves blown along the ground by the chill October wind. His dog had vanished!

Tyler eased out on the rough grey stone, trying to see into the thick woods. The trees still held half or more of their bright fall foliage. He cupped a hand to his mouth and called again, "Here, Rachel!" Then he heard a faint, excited barking from the depths of the forest.

Rachel! Was she in trouble?

"Grandpa, it's Rachel." Tyler called to the man coming along the path toward his rock. "Hear her barking? I think she needs help. Let's get down there."

"Hold on, Tyler." Grandpa Turner chuckled as he stepped up beside his grandson. "Little old Rachel is a city dog. She's probably just treed a squirrel and doesn't know what to do about it. Why, she can't even find her way home after one day in the country."

Seeing the worried frown on Tyler's upturned face, the farmer quickly added, "Come on. We'll check her out, just in case." Tyler was looking toward the distant sound of the dog and missed the twinkle in his grandfather's brown eyes.

"I don't think it's a squirrel, Grandpa. I've never heard her bark so fast before." And without waiting for an answer, the boy jumped to the ground. Grandpa quickly followed.

The two picked their way down the faint path, probably an animal trail, which angled back and forth across the steep face of the rock. Several times one or the other slipped on small stones. As they grabbed at bushes and tree branches to keep from falling, loosened rocks and clumps of dirt clattered into the dim glade below them.

Near the lower edge of the trail, Tyler tripped and tumbled into the base of a thick tree. A mass of leaves and sticks cushioned his fall so that he wasn't hurt, but Grandpa scrambled down the rocky slope to the boy.

Tyler sat up, grinning. "Did you see that, Grandpa? Boy! I bet I did two turns in the air! Bet you couldn't do that."

"No, Son, you're right. I couldn't do that fall if you paid me. Here . . . let's have a look." Grandpa quickly ran his expert hands over Tyler's lanky body to check for injuries and then ruffled his hair. "Well, you're mighty lucky."

Tyler bounced to his feet. "Come on, Grandpa! We've got to see about Rachel." He ran toward the deeper forest, kicking up little showers of red and gold leaves. Shaking his head and chuckling again to himself, Grandpa jogged after him.

Much nearer now but still down the hill in the

woods beyond, the shrill barking continued. All about them, fallen logs and rocks jutted from the shaded hillside. Under their feet twigs and small branches cracked and snapped. "Watch your feet, Son. Don't want you falling twice, do we?" Grandpa called.

When they reached the larger trees, they paused to look around. A startled quail flew up on noisy, beating wings.

Peering intently into the shade, Tyler saw a small black-and-white figure some distance away. He and Grandpa ran toward it. The animal was dashing back and forth around a large oak, leaping at the trunk and yelping excitedly.

"Rachel! Rachel! What are you doing, girl?" Tyler called as he neared the dog.

Ignoring the boy and the man, Rachel kept up her leaping and yelping.

Grandpa chortled and slapped Tyler on his shoulder. "Just as I thought. She doesn't know what to do about these country squirrels. See that hole in the tree. They're too fast for her."

"Oh, Rachel," a slightly embarrassed Tyler muttered as he threw himself down beside the excited dog. She turned and leaped on him, licking his face. Her wagging tail thumped his side. "Well, that's okay. At least you knew they were squirrels." Tyler grinned up at his grandpa.

Tyler was happy, and he knew Rachel was too. Both boy and dog had arrived yesterday for a visit. He and his family often came to the Ozark farm of his grandparents at Thanksgiving and Christmas, but he had never been able to stay as long as he wanted in these beautiful Missouri hills—and never by himself. And now he and his dog were here for a whole week!

Tyler stood up. "How far is it to the river, Grandpa?"

"It's a little ways on down these woods." They turned to go and the little dog bounded forward, running ahead of them.

After a few minutes of walking, Tyler saw a glint of sparkling light between the rocks and through the big trees ahead. The river! He ran toward it with Rachel in the lead.

Coming up to the edge of the swift stream behind Rachel who was drinking, Tyler threw a rock. Even above the sound of the current, Rachel heard the splash and jumped away. Both Tyler and his grandfather laughed as they watched her race for the trees, nose snuffing the rich earth.

"The river's not too big now," Grandpa said, over the sound of the water, "but you should see it in the spring. Tons of icy water rush through here, tumbling these big old rocks over each other. You wouldn't believe it, would you? Why, you couldn't get this far down this steep valley at all. Come on. Let's go along the bank a ways.

"This is the St. Francis," Grandpa explained as he and Tyler stepped onto and around the rocks. "Time was, years and years ago, it was the only easy way into these hills. I guess you'd call it a mountain highway. Indians were all around then—Osage, Shawnee, Sac, Delaware. All of them used the river. Wasn't much good at times for their canoes—too rocky and fast, like here, and too narrow in other spots. But they walked the banks, the little valley, and especially the ridges above us." He pointed upward to the high rim of limestone that could be seen through the overhanging trees growing close to the river's edge.

"When the Osage were here, they fought everyone. Even a long time after they left for the West, they figured this was their hunting grounds and came back from time to time. They were mostly big fellows, brave and plenty smart."

They tramped along a bit more in silence. Then Grandpa asked, "You know we have Cherokee blood in us, don't you?"

Tyler nodded, his wide eyes watching his grandfather's deeply tanned face. Yes, he believed it.

"Well, history says there were a few Cherokee living in this very valley as far back as 1785, though I don't know as our ancestor was around then. No white people lived right here either. Just a few fur trappers once in a while."

Grandpa paused a moment and pointed. "Look at all those old crows." In the treetops near the river Tyler saw dozens of crows. They were black against the golden leaves, skimming and dipping as they restlessly flew from one perch to another. Their noisy squabbling sounded over the rush of the water at his feet.

And then Tyler saw the tree! The vivid orange and gold top of a curiously shaped old tree shot at least forty feet high.

"Grandpa. Look at that strange tree. Did something mash it over when it was little?"

Grandpa stepped higher on the rocks beside the stream to see the bent tree better.

"Well, well, would you look at that," Grandpa whispered, almost to himself. He stood staring, lost in thought. Then he turned to Tyler. "Nope, I guess not.

16

Nature didn't smash that old tree. Leastwise, I don't think so."

Tyler looked from the strange tree to the silent man.

"What is it, Grandpa? Is it something special?" Tyler pressed.

"Yes, Tyler, it is. It sure is. It's a thong tree, an Indian thong tree. I've seen only one other in these parts." He shook his head in wonder.

"What kind of tree, Grandpa?"

"Indian message tree made from a hickory. It's been here a long, long time. Come on. Let's get closer for a look."

Tyler scrambled eagerly from the rocks to the leaf-packed bank, ran through the weeds to the old bent tree, and put his hands on the rough trunk. Grandpa followed, all the while looking up at the ancient tree.

Reaching with his arms, Tyler couldn't quite circle the hickory where it left the ground. When he stood next to the tree, his head was even with the flat bend which angled away from the trunk. The bark was scarred and flattened at each of the bends. The straight piece was more than seven feet long, Grandpa guessed. Like a great flower, the rest of the tree jumped into the sky, its branches brilliant with fall color.

"There's a story in our family tells of a young Chero-kee scout who made such trees as this, and maybe in these same hills too. It's a strange thing . . . us finding this tree like we did . . ." Grandpa's voice trailed off as he stared at the bent tree.

Tyler pulled his eyes from his grandfather's quiet face and tilted his head toward the bent hickory. "Could that

old tree be one of his, Grandpa? Who was he? Why did he bend it? How did—"

The boy stopped his questions and dropped to the ground, watching his grandfather's brown muscular hands as they lightly brushed the old trunk. Rachel darted back and forth into the brush close by, tongue out, tail wagging.

Grandpa didn't answer Tyler's question directly. "A forest has been here for thousands of years, always thick, I'd guess, around the river yonder. And this hickory is mighty old too, maybe a hundred and fifty or sixty years. See how the flat part of its trunk points up-river?" Grandpa waved his hand northward, then slapped it down on the hickory tree. "Probably shows a good crossing spot."

Tyler looked up the river. "Grandpa—"

The man shrugged away the boy's probable question and lowered himself against the gnarled hickory. Shifting to find the most comfortable position, Grandpa paused to rub his chin—a gesture, Tyler had learned, that often led to good stories.

"My grandma told me that her great-grandma, a full-blooded Cherokee named Morning Fire, or something like that, had a brother who was a warrior-scout. This must have been sometime in the early 1800s maybe."

Grandpa Turner was quiet for a moment. "Well, any-way, it seems this scout—I can't now recall his name—had the job of going ahead to find the best trails and watering places for a small bunch of them. Seems they were moving to a nicer place they'd heard of. This scout was pretty far ahead all the time and he had to be cer-tain whatever message he left would be understood.

19

So, he bent trees like this, knowing they'd be spotted right off."

"How did he bend them?"

"I'll get to that in good time. . . . But other things happened and this scout's life was in danger. At least, I don't think my grandma was fooling me when she told me it was nip and tuck with the young scout—er— Runs-to-Earth. That's it. That's what she called him."

Grandpa's words formed bright mental images for Tyler. He peered into the growing shadows under the trees. He could almost picture a young Cherokee running through the hills, perhaps these very woods.

CHAPTER

2

The Cherokee Scout

Runs-to-Earth came at a trot, head moving, dark eyes searching his surroundings. Up from the river, he was wet from splashing across the rocky ford. His one-piece moccasins squished as his feet lightly touched the ground.

In a wooded cove to his left, he found a tiny trickle of clear water burbling from a rock outcropping. Oak and hickory saplings grew among the large pines, and fragrant grasses hid the dark, rocky earth.

Working swiftly, Runs-to-Earth gathered tiny, dry twigs and grouped them into a little cone on a bare spot of ground near the stream. From a leather pouch hanging at his side, he took flint and steel and a palm-sized bit of dry punk he'd saved from the inner part of a dry, rotting log. Putting a piece of the punk under the twigs, he struck a spark into it from the flint and steel. In a moment or two, a thread of smoke was curling upward from the punk he had gently coaxed into fire. The flames, sheltered from any distant eyes, soon gave a welcome warmth with very little smoke.

He dumped the fire tools and remaining punk into

the strike-a-light pouch. Next, he shrugged the quiver and pouch from his shoulders and let them fall at his feet. The rolled blanket he also carried fell with them. Sitting, he drew off his drenched moccasins, squeezed them tightly under his arms, and stuffed them full of dry grass. He laid them near the fire, but not too near for fear that they would dry rapidly and shrink. They were his only pair.

Night came rapidly and quietly. Overhead, the stars appeared. Moving into the shadows away from the little fire, he wrapped the blanket about himself and tucked it under his feet. He began to chew a piece of jerky he'd taken from another pouch. Alert to all night sounds, he chewed slowly, eyes never looking directly at the fire but probing the dark around him. Others who were not his brothers might be roaming this forest.

After a time he rose, slipped over to the water, knelt, and drank deeply. Next, he bent and pulled the largest sticks from the fire's center. He felt his moccasins for wetness. Then he moved farther into the cove, well away from the dying light of the fire. With his broad-bladed knife he scraped shallow trenches in the earth for his shoulders and hips and piled pine boughs and grasses in them. Wrapped tightly in the blanket, he lay upon his crude bed, his weapons close to his hand.

A gentle wind stirred the embers of the fire. Whip-poorwills called and an owl screeched in the dark trees. Over the wooded ridge a wolf began his yipping song. Others of his kind took it up until a chorus was formed, their voices blending before their nightly hunt.

Long before first light poked over the hills, the scout was awake. He lay very still, listening, moving only his eyes, letting them grow accustomed to the heavy

shadows. All seemed well so Runs-to-Earth quickly stood, threw off his blanket, and stretched. He drank from the cold stream, then for breakfast, chewed several pieces of jerky. When he had finished, he ran his hands over the crown of his head and down his braided hair.

He removed the damp grass wadding from his almost-dry moccasins and pulled them on his feet. After dousing the grey ashes with a few palmsful of water, he carefully brushed dirt over the fire spot until he was satisfied no other eyes would find it. He threw the wadding, grasses, and pine boughs around in the brush so they looked as though they had long lain there. He replaced the dirt in his sleeping place just as he had in the fire spot. No sign of his passage must remain.

Almost all of Runs-to-Earth's morning tasks were finished. He had only to leave the marker tree for his people before pushing on. They would need to know the direction he was traveling and how far it was to the next safe river crossing. He snatched up his small hatchet and ducked quickly into the bush.

After he had cut two long, very stout forked branches from oak saplings, he pounded one of them deep into the ground, quite close to the trunk of a small hickory tree. With a quick leap he grasped an upper branch of the hickory and pulled the top earthward, his muscles taut with the effort. Then carefully, so as not to crack it, he bent the tree over the fork.

Leaning one powerful arm over the bent trunk, he held it in place while he wrapped and tied rawhide thongs to bind the tree and the oak fork together. Then he held onto the bent hickory and moved farther along

the tree's trunk, perhaps seven feet toward the leafy top, where he pinned it with the other oak fork. He pounded this firmly into the ground with his hatchet. Again, he bound the two different woods with rawhide. Finally, he lopped off the top of the hickory, leaving only one side branch shooting up toward the sky. He stepped back to check the angle of the pinned tree. It pointed straight to the river crossing. His marker was complete.

Suddenly, he froze in a crouch and jerked his eyes in the direction of the river and its towering bluffs. Every muscle taut, the red-brown man was alert, waiting. He replaced his hatchet with one hand while the other moved slowly to his knife.

In the awakening woods, birds chirped drowsily, a fox barked, a turkey clucked in the dense underbrush. Grey fingers of early fog drifted over the rocks and lightly touched the trees.

The Cherokee swung his attention up the hill through the woods. Had the large Osage found him? Were those dogs here, those killers of women and children, scourge of the prairies? His heart thudded in his chest. For ten long breaths he listened, moving no muscle.

A second turkey clucked in answer to the first. The thinning fog continued to drift through the cove. Tiny drops of sweat glimmered on Runs-to-Earth's forehead, his cheeks, and his upper lip. He drew another breath before he moved. One thing was certain—he had to get away fast.

3

The Thong Tree

Tyler was disappointed when his grandfather pushed himself off the hard ground and grunted.

"You aren't finished, are you, Grandpa? What about the tree? Were there other Indians around?"

"Hold on, hold on, boy. One thing at a time. I just got tired sitting here and I figured to show you how that scout must have made the tree. You do want to see, don't you?"

"You bet!" Tyler leaped to his feet and Rachel danced beside him. Grandpa was bending over for a long stick with a fork at the end. Then he motioned to Tyler.

"Come here and help me with this sapling."

Grandpa had his hands on a small hickory shoot, perhaps ten feet in height. It was growing close to the old thong tree.

"Here, you take hold of the upper end there and bend it until it's parallel with the ground."

Tyler jumped and grabbed the leafy top of the sapling. He pulled it toward the earth, thinking the wood might crack any moment, but it didn't. Grandpa took hold of it and Tyler stepped back.

"You see, the Indian would place a very stout forked stick—it's called a thong—right here by the trunk. Now, out toward the top, he'd push another forked thong over the sapling, pinning it down. And both of these thongs he'd pound into the ground to make certain the little tree stayed bent over. After a while it grew into that shape. While he had the little thing down, he might cut off the top close to the last thong he'd put in—all the top, that is, except maybe he'd choose one good, healthy side branch pointing toward the sky and he'd leave that. In time, as the sapling grew, the side branch would become the main upright trunk—like our old hickory thong tree over there. We can let the little thing up now. We won't really thong it. We've no reason to change its nature, have we?"

Tyler laughed as, with a breezy swish, the tiny hickory reset itself, golden leaves shaking. A few, too dry to hang on longer, fluttered to the ground. The boy walked the short distance to the ancient hickory and looked up into its high branches.

"But what does this tree say, Grandpa? What message was the scout leaving?"

"Course, we don't really know, but I'm guessing it was something like, 'Keep to the high ground this side of the river. Avoid the rocky bluffs.' Or maybe, 'Keep heading this way. Good water and safe camping ahead.' There is another thong tree quite a ways off, between this one and a bend in the river. That's the only other one I've ever seen. Maybe there're more over the next few ridges and hills. I don't know."

Squatting to tie his shoelaces, Tyler asked, "Were the Osage behind the scout? Did your grandma know?"

"I don't know if she *knew* for certain, but she did tell

28

me a story. Come on down to the river again. I'll show you something."

When they had pushed through the thick stand of volunteer sycamore shoots to reach the water's edge, Tyler saw that the St. Francis River was broken here with small rapids. On the far bank was a high, rocky bluff with numerous dark openings. Small trees and brushy shrubs jutted from several cracks on the nearly vertical face of the brownish-white rock. The bluff extended upstream with large boulders along its base. High on top was a dense growth of huge oaks and other trees whose red leaves were now glowing from the low, slanting rays of the falling sun. The reflection of this light, seen in the waters of the St. Francis below, made the pools above the rapids appear to be filled with blood.

Grandpa peered through the treetops at gathering clouds. Gusts of damp, chill air blew down the canyon.

Raising his voice to be heard over the noisy river, Grandpa pointed to the face of the bluff. "My grandma told me the scout hid in a rocky cave. She never said where. Maybe up there?" He said this last as a question to himself.

"From the Osage?"

"Yep, from the Osage. He felt they were close. So, after thonging the tree, he packed up and left in a hurry!"

4

The Scalp Hunters

Runs-to-Earth slipped the hide loops of his deerskin quivers over his shoulder and pulled them high on his back. Shoving the folded blanket under the quiver loops, he dashed up the wooded slope into the deep shadows.

Alarmed at the sudden motion, a small rabbit skipped nervously into a blackberry thicket. Growing light from the east filtered through the forest, adding a golden tint to the darkness under the trees. A strange hush as before a storm settled over the place of the little thong tree. Time passed and the early morning light faded behind building rain clouds.

Six painted, half-naked men stepped quietly into the clearing that Runs-to-Earth had left not long before. Tall and straight they were, these Indian strangers. Only a center scalp lock topped their bald, shiny heads.

One of them dropped to his knees by the little stream, thrust his green-and-yellow-striped face into the water, and drank. Two others looked about and at the same moment spotted the newly thonged hickory shoot. They began excitedly "talking" with their hands.

As those around him gestured, the tallest of the group watched with slit eyes, then pulled a wood-handled knife from his belt sash. He held it before his sweaty chest and gently ran his left thumb along its keen edge. The corners of his wide mouth suddenly tilted up, making him appear more wolf than man. The others in the hunting party knew this grin. Thrusting the knife into his belt, he stopped the others with a few signs. "Enough! Quickly—before the rains that come wash it away—find the trail of this creeper of the east, this dog we seek."

He paused, looked at the others, and then made a savage, down-slashing movement of his right arm. "If it be fresh as I think, then we shall have him! Hau! His scalp shall dry before my fire. Find him!"

Carefully casting about from the tiny thong tree like dogs smelling for rabbits, the Osage covered the earth and the brush. Then, a triumphant grunt from one warrior called the others to crowd around a faint moccasin impression in the soil. A quick gesture, a muscular arm thrust in a northerly direction, several grunts in response, and the six figures sprang away.

Across the slope of the hill they ran, easily following the track. They knew the Cherokee had been running because of the length of his stride. Once or twice they spotted a heel print or saw a bit of overturned grass and dirt.

Thunder rumbled through the river canyon. Lightning flashed.

And from his cave high in the bluffs across the river, Runs-to-Earth saw them flitting through the distant forest like ghosts. He'd known the tall killers were trailing him. He'd known by trusting his feelings. He always did. Early this morning he'd felt them coming for him.

So he deliberately left a false trail to the big bend of the river, over a ridge and a steep hill—perhaps an hour's run north. He'd faked his footprints going into the river and out the other side too, as though he were still running away. Then he had stepped backward in his tracks to the river—an old trick but one that required great care—entered the cold, rushing water, and waded back downstream to a spot just below the cave in the bluff. The water was fast and powerful. He had almost been swept under more than once, and he'd had to hurry.

His heart was still hammering as he lay in the cave. Every muscle in his body quivered with strain and weariness. How close he had come to being seen! If those Osage warriors had only looked up, across the river and toward the high bluffs, even in the failing light they would have seen him clinging to roots and branches growing from the rocky wall. By the time he'd reached the cave opening, sweat stung his eyes and dripped off his nose.

The narrow cave in which he lay had been used by animals. Dry bones of various sizes and shapes littered the rocky, uneven floor. Patches of fur were here and there. A stale, musty smell hung in the air. Outside, a slow, steady rain fell.

Lying in his wet garments, he stared out the tiny cave opening and thought of his situation. Even if the killers found that he'd tricked them and waded the river back to here, they would have great difficulty reaching him, high as he was. And he would make them pay a great price if they did!

Time passed. He was cold but he slept lightly, gathering his strength.

Down below the Osage who was running in the lead slowed, looked around, then trotted cautiously from the edge of the timber to the river. He was quickly joined by the others. Two of the warriors splashed across the cold, foamy water, slipping several times on rocks that rolled under their feet. On the opposite side, they immediately saw the deep moccasin prints in the muddy, clay bank. Clearly, the Cherokee was heading northwest toward a range of steep hills covered with thick forest. They signaled this to the leader across the river.

He gestured in turn, "You follow with care. We remain here for a time to know if he has truly left us."

Into the grey rain the two vanished from sight. The remaining four moved along the rocky banks, two heading upstream and two working their way downstream . . . toward the Cherokee's cave hideaway.

Falling faster now, the rain dimmed Runs-to-Earth's view of the hunt being carried out by his enemies along the river below. Where were they? Had they discovered his trick?

Water poured down the face of the bluff and spattered into the opening in spite of the slight rock ledge over the cave mouth. He was cold and wet but he dared not build a fire, even if he'd had room for one. Though the Osage might not see any smoke because of the rain, they would smell it. He could not risk it. They must believe he had escaped already!

Runs-to-Earth looked to the care of his weapons. He might need them quite soon. He thrust the bowcase and quiver of arrows far back in the rock niche to keep them as dry as possible. Otherwise, the bowstring and the sinew thread bindings would stretch from the damp and the weapons would be useless.

Again, he looked from the cave to the river below. He spotted the two Osage working their way along the edge, among the rocks near the base of his bluff cave. But where were the rest of them? He crawled cautiously forward to peer over the cave's rim.

The two Osage standing in the heavy downpour at the base of the bluff, heads tilted upward, eyes almost closed against the rain, looked for signs of the Cherokee. There were none. The water streaming down the wall had washed them away. The younger turned to the other. "What now, my brother? Should we scale this height seeking the cowardly scout?"

The other, still looking at the rocky wall above them, was silent for a time. He spoke at last. "My medicine says that misfortune lies this way. I do not like the look of this cliff. Besides, I think it unlikely he would have courage enough to remain so close to us."

The pair searched a bit farther along the river before turning upstream, not far from the bluff, to rejoin their fierce leader. The two who had set off northward through the forest had also returned. They had lost the faint trail in the rain. All six men huddled under a sycamore overhanging the bank.

In council, standing under the dripping tree, each gave his opinion as to the whereabouts of the Cherokee. Five did not believe he was still nearby.

With a voice full of menace, the leader spoke last. "Hear me! It is late and the rain still falls heavily. It would be useless to seek further this day. When Sun appears on the morrow, we will search again! My belief is strong that he hides close about. We will set watch through the night."

His eyes mere slits, the big man placed both hands over his flat belly. He glared intently at each of his followers. All were silent. None dared to question him.

"I do not think he will escape," he rumbled.

"Hau's" of agreement came from the other throats.

At the leader's impatient gesture, the five rose and began erecting a temporary brush-and-sapling shelter. Quickly they pulled together several young trees over their heads and tied them with a few buckskin cords. Over this dome-shaped wickiup they piled as many branches with leaves still attached as they could gather. Though the ground underneath was soggy and water still dripped through, they soon had a warming fire in the temporary lodge. The smoke drifted low in the wet air.

And the faint scent of burning wood carried on the wind down the canyon, warning Runs-to-Earth—the Osage still hunted!

5

A Long, Dark Run

A sharp blast of thunder over the hills made Tyler jump. Big splatters of rain fell from the almost-dark sky. Rachel ran to cower beside him, her tail tucked between her legs.

"We'd better go—now!" exclaimed Grandpa, jumping quickly off the high rock toward the river bank. A large stone rolled under his feet. He fell to the ground with a small cry, clutching his booted right foot.

"Grandpa!" Tyler shouted.

Rushing to his side, Tyler helped his grandfather sit up. Grandpa Turner still held his foot tightly in both hands. Pain wrinkled his tanned face and he rocked back and forth, breathing deeply.

"Must be sprained. I think I felt something pull. Hmmm—wow!" he grunted at last. "Can you help me get to my good foot, Tyler?"

Tyler's stomach churned to see his grandfather in pain. He stepped close, held out both hands, and helped Grandpa pull himself erect. Rain was now falling hard and fast and soaking their clothing. Tyler shivered. Rachel scooted under dense brush near the woods.

"Full dark will come quick now," Grandpa declared, still breathing heavily and leaning against Tyler.

Blue-white lightning flashed in the sky behind the high bluff and thunder instantly ripped through the river canyon.

Looking anxiously around, Tyler yelled, "What are we going to do, Grandpa? Can you walk if I help?"

Again, thunder blasted the air. Once more, Tyler jumped, his shaking arms still helping Grandpa to stand.

"Not likely," cried Grandpa. "Besides, that'd take a long time and your grandma'll be upset."

Tyler understood at once. Grandpa was hurting far worse than he would admit.

"You could trot on out, Tyler, see Grandma before she gets too anxious, ask her to bring the truck—"

"How will I find my way? I don't know the way back, Grandpa. You know that." Tyler's voice was tight. His upper lip trembled. He felt his grandfather's hand patting his shoulder.

When Grandpa spoke, his voice was calm but tinged with pain. "Son, don't try going back over the hills. The surest way home is to follow the river. Stay with it—be careful on the rocky banks, though. It'll take you to an old logging trail, mostly overgrown now, but you'll know it."

"How, Grandpa, how—"

"You'll see it close to where an old game and Indian path crosses the St. Francis. It's pretty plain. And look about for that other thong tree I mentioned. You'll know it now. Turn left about there—away from the river—and stay on the logging trail to my north field. Climb over the fence and head across the pasture away from the hill. The house isn't far then. You'll see the lights—you can do it!" Grandpa gripped Tyler's shoulder and smiled encouragingly. Cold water ran off their heads and down their faces.

"I guess so, Grandpa." Tyler tried to sound more courageous than he felt. The truth was, he was afraid. Grandpa knew it too.

"Where'll you be, Grandpa? How'll we find you?" Thinking about his grandfather and not himself helped Tyler.

"Now don't you fret, Tyler. Grandma'll figure out how to get me. This vest will keep me warm. Off with you—we don't want her worrying too much. AND BE CAREFUL!"

Waving once, Tyler began to run, Rachel at his side. Except for following the river, he wasn't sure he could remember Grandpa's directions. He was scared he'd miss the logging trail. What if he didn't find the thong tree in the dark? Grandpa said the trail met the river where the Indians once crossed. . . . If he didn't find it, he'd be lost! Fright gathered in his chest, then settled in a big knot in his belly.

Rachel ran close at his heels as lightning suddenly brightened the woods. The bolt was accompanied by a roar of thunder. Cold rain dashed Tyler's face and flattened his hair. He could hear the rushing river at his right.

The boy and dog hurried on. Tyler was drenched and slipping often as he swerved to avoid a huge rock or a downed tree limb in his path. He took deep breaths and thought of Grandpa's foot. And then he remembered Runs-to-Earth.

Yes, Grandpa's story was now very real to him. For,

somewhere in these woods, so many years ago, his Cherokee ancestor had laid a thong tree trail—and then had run for his life! As Tyler thought of it, a prickly feeling swept over him and his breath caught in his throat. How must it feel to be hunted on a night such as this, in these lonely woods—hunted by the Osage. . . .

Running faster now, Tyler leaped over an old log. Underbrush whipped around him as he sped by. The center of his back tensed as he imagined he felt the touch of a searching hand.

Rachel growled once, and Tyler redoubled his efforts, his scalp prickling again.

Weariness, however, finally won. He slowed to a walk, then stopped, gasping for air, chest heaving, a stitch in his side. In spite of his long run, Tyler shivered in his light clothing.

Above, a freshening wind was quickly thinning the racing clouds, and the rain had slacked. The October storm was passing away.

"Come on, Rachel," he croaked after resting a few moments. "We'd better keep moving."

The two pushed on under still-dripping trees to more level ground. In a few minutes of fast walking, they reached a clearing where the high grass slowed their pace a bit. Faint moonlight defined the shapes of trees and rocks.

When he had almost crossed the clearing, Tyler suddenly halted, staring ahead. The other thong tree! They'd found it! There it was, the same strange bent shape—but a far bigger tree than the old hickory down in the valley. It stood apart from the other trees on the edge of the clearing. Gnarled and black, it was pointing as though Runs-to-Earth himself stood there.

44

"Rachel," Tyler shouted, "that's the way to the house! Let's go!" And they began to run again in the direction shown by the ancient tree.

Past the thong tree and down a little hill, Tyler burst through dripping underbrush to an overgrown trail. He came to it so quickly that he skidded on the wet ground and fell hard. For a moment he lay still, then he got to his feet, rubbing his right leg and knee briskly. "I'm okay, girl. We'd better go on."

They set off again at a trot down the weed-choked trail. A turn somewhere beyond should lead them to the field not far from the house . . .

Grandpa was right!

Ahead, Tyler spotted the cedar posts of the fence. He slowed to a walk so as not to run into the barbed wire he knew was there. Then he slipped safely between the rusty strands and started across the field, away from the dark woods. Rachel darted in front and was quickly lost to view, but her sharp barks echoed back to him.

Suddenly Tyler saw lights and quickened his pace. A moment passed before he realized the lights were moving. Then he heard the motor over Rachel's excited yelping. It was Grandpa's pickup truck wallowing slowly across the rutted field. Rachel was in the lead, darting in and out of the lights moving toward him. Relieved, and a little weak, Tyler waved his arms and shouted.

"Here! Here I am, Grandma! Over here."

6

The Osage Trap

In time, night fell and the rain stopped. Seeing the faintest glow of a fire from upriver, the Cherokee knew the Osage were alert. He must leave when darkness was absolute. Otherwise, tomorrow would end very differently than had this day.

There was only one possible way out for him—through the forest at the top of the bluff. With the Osage warriors watching the other side of the river and its crossing spot, he had no other choice.

Now the question: how could he get to the top? He must think on this . . .

Shortly, in the black silence the answer came. Of course! The animal that used this cave last, probably a cougar or a wildcat, had to have come in from above. No four-footed creature could come up from below; he'd seen that. Some kind of path must descend to the cave!

Runs-to-Earth's spirits lifted, and he carefully twisted around in his narrow space to run his hands over the bluff face outside. He must be very quiet. No stone or stick must fall. Fortunately, dark clouds still covered the sky. The river was very noisy with fresh runoff from the rain.

His hands scrabbled over the rock above the cave. Out to the side, then up, over, and up again. His back hurt from the rough edge of the stone. Small hunks of mud and dirt, loosened by his groping fingers, blinded him for a moment. Quickly, he stopped to wipe his eyes. Still they burned and he blinked rapidly to clear them. Then his hands were moving again, fingers exploring.

There it was—a small and very slippery rock shelf jutting from the bluff beyond the cave opening. It was above the roof of his small hiding place. Good! This must be the way. He would go!

Reaching into the back of the cave, Runs-to-Earth pulled forth his bow and arrow quivers and carefully tied them so they would hang from his belt. Once that was done, he took a deep breath, paused, then hooked his fingers into the rock roof, squirmed forward with his legs, and slid out. Reaching up and across for the jutting rock, he pulled himself—slowly, carefully—until he could stand, barely perched on the narrow shelf. His upper body was pressed tightly against the wet, cold stone of the bluff. Only once did he allow himself to think of the rocky blackness below.

Holding with one hand, he explored with the other and discovered a second shelf above and to his right. Using only his arms, he pulled himself so that first a foot, then a knee could lift him. Once balanced on the second and wider shelf, he caught his breath and relaxed his arms.

His Above-Helpers had shown him the way to these ledges. Surely they would remain to guide him to safety! He must continue to be brave and strong of heart.

In the inky dark he set himself to search again. And he found another ledge, the largest yet. Confidently he began to raise himself when suddenly the rock in his right hand wrenched loose and fell, hitting below with a clattering crash! His body jerked rigid and he swayed outward for an instant before his hand seized a rocky projection. He pulled himself in to the bluff and hugged it.

His heart pumped violently, and his limbs trembled. In spite of the chill air, sweat poured from him. If he had needed further proof of the power of his Above-Helpers, he had just had it. Without their aid, he would now be crushed and broken.

Had the noise of the falling stone carried to his unseen enemies? Was he discovered? He dared not linger. Having no other choice, he forced himself to continue the fearful climb.

Many long minutes passed until, muscles in agony, the weary young Cherokee's arms reached over the lip of the bluff and pressed into wet grass and sharp rocks. His escape was almost complete. He managed a big heave and rolled his body onto the grass, away from the edge of the cliff.

Panting, Runs-to-Earth lay for a moment, then rose shakily to his feet. Knowing he was still in great danger, he gathered his remaining strength, hurriedly felt for his weapons, and pushed his way up the slope. The black forest was just ahead.

He stopped and crouched at the margin of the woods. He saw nothing and heard nothing. All was quiet—perhaps too quiet. It was unnaturally still.

He pulled his knife from his belt and stood. With great care he moved through the heavy undergrowth until he found a small path, a game trail. Turning to his left, he broke into a trot. His feet made only a whisper in the night.

Suddenly, Runs-to-Earth was struck from behind and thrown violently forward, something huge riding his back.

OSAGE! The thought flashed into his mind just as he rammed into the ground and his head exploded with millions of bright stars and lights. A muscular arm locked around his throat, pulling his head back, back. Powerful legs encircled his, clamping them tightly together. He was stunned. Air to his lungs was almost squeezed off, his mind was dimming . . . going blank . . . a mist seemed to be gathering in front of his eyes.

Pure reflex caused the Cherokee to strike with his knife at the other body next to him. Once, twice, his right arm slashed and plunged, drew back and plunged again.

An explosive "Huh!" burst from the Osage as his body jerked. The arm around Runs-to-Earth's neck tightened savagely, then slowly relaxed. A final time, the young scout plunged his blade into the Osage. A moment later, his enemy lay still. Panting, exhausted, the Cherokee pulled free from the dead Osage and crawled slowly away.

For a little while, Runs-to-Earth sat in silence, head down, gathering his strength. Then he pulled himself together, got to his feet, and once more set off into the night forest, heading northward.

He was free. His people depended upon his trail. He would not be caught by the Osage!

Tyler Learns a Secret

The blue truck, now pinning Tyler in its lights, jolted to a stop just in front of him. Blinking in the bright glare, he heard the driver's door bang open and Grandma's anxious voice.

"Tyler! Tyler! Are you all right? You must be cold. Where's Grandpa? Is he hurt? Come . . . get in the truck. Rachel too."

Tyler slid onto the worn seat, helping Rachel in behind him. He was grateful for the warmth in the cab. Then he found he couldn't answer all Grandma's questions at once.

"Yes, Grandma . . . no, Grandma . . . I'm okay, Grandma, really. Grandpa's hurt—but he's going to be okay too." Tyler rushed to add, "Once we get him home." Then he remembered Grandpa's warning not to alarm Grandma, just have her bring the truck.

But he needn't have been concerned about Grandma. She promptly handed him a big towel to dry his hair with. She had him remove his soaked jacket and shirt and wrap himself in a thick blanket she'd brought. Without asking, she knew he was tired, and probably hungry as well. Just before setting the truck in motion again, she fished around in a paper sack at her feet and handed Tyler a sandwich. Grandma Turner, Tyler proudly realized, was a lady who didn't panic easily.

Keeping her eyes riveted through the dark windshield, she slowly steered the truck over rutted fields, through a break in the wire fence, and onto the grass-filled logging track. All the while, Tyler, bouncing on the seat and stuffing his mouth with his sandwich, related his story of the past several hours. From her practical questions, he learned that Grandma knew where the logging road led and even had an idea where Grandpa was.

"Yes, I remember being over on that side of the hill with your grandfather, but, my, it's been years."

But the hickory thong tree was a surprise. She had heard Grandpa talk only of the one near the river bend he'd found a long time ago. She listened quietly as Tyler relived his terror of running along the river. He didn't mention, though, fearing an imagined Osage was after him.

And then he told her of finding the second old thong tree, just as Grandpa had said he would. It had pointed his way to the logging trail.

"I knew I could make it then," Tyler added proudly. "It was as though the Cherokee was there too."

"Maybe he was there, Tyler, maybe he was. Old Grandma Turner told some curious stories about that Indian . . ." Her voice faded away. Tyler looked at her in the dim light of the cab.

The truck slowly climbed the overgrown road, bumping over rocks, and now and then sliding in the wet weeds and mud. As she drove, Grandma told Tyler that the storm had knocked out electric power to the house. She said she'd waited quite a while for them to return but had finally set out in the truck to look for them. She had an idea there might have been trouble. The third time she went around the big pasture, she'd spotted Rachel.

"I just turned the truck around and followed her, and there you were too."

At that moment Tyler saw a brownish-grey animal slip through their headlights and vanish into the dark woods alongside the narrow, rutted track.

"Coyote!" exclaimed Grandma, intent on her driving.

The boy shivered. They had been in the woods with him too. Just as wolves had been with Runs-to-Earth. So many things he and his remote ancestor seemed to share—these hills, the thong trees, animals in the night, a storm, terror in the woods. He thought of it all as they pushed on through the weedy growth.

Once, Tyler and Grandma had to get out and struggle to drag aside a log. Later, at another log, Grandma drove around it, turning the bouncing truck through the edge of the woods. The tires spun, churning and throwing big clumps of weeds and mud. Tyler thought they would surely bog down but Grandma just shifted into a lower gear and on they went.

Shortly, she turned into a second, more rutted track. Now they were jolting along a rocky ridge.

"Not far ahead is where I think you and Grandpa were. We'll stop, blow the horn, and see if he hollers to us."

Tyler was about to ask how they could possibly get

Grandpa up the slope to the truck when they rounded another sharp bend. And there, framed in their bright lights, stood his grandfather. He was mud-spattered and wet, and he leaned heavily on a stick. Shielding his eyes from the glare, he waved an arm.

"Grandpa," shouted Tyler, wrenching open his door and tumbling out before Grandma had braked the truck. He ran to greet the muddy figure and threw his arms about his grandfather. Rachel barked from the back of the truck.

"Grandpa! Are you okay? How'd you get here? How's—?"

"Not so fast," Grandpa chuckled as Grandma joined them. She gave him a quick kiss and he leaned on her as he hobbled to the truck. "I just poked up that hill with my stick, slow and easy. I had a lot of time."

At the truck he gave Grandma a long hug and then leaned against the seat as she bent to look at his foot.

"Can't tell anything until we get that boot off. What does it feel like, Richard?"

"Well, it's a bad sprain but not broken, Helen," Grandpa replied, trying to disguise his own concern. "We'll see." He looked at Tyler. "Glad you're okay, young man. I was a little worried about you." He squeezed his grandson's arm.

"Come on, you two." Grandma said. "Get in the truck. I want to get home where I can see that foot." She moved to help Grandpa up into the cab. Tyler shifted from one foot to another, ready if they needed him.

Once settled in the cab with Rachel sitting on his lap, Tyler, almost shyly, asked, "Grandpa? What did happen to Runs-to-Earth? Did he get away?"

"Why, didn't I tell you, Son? Yes, he escaped that

night. My grandma told me the Cherokee climbed the rock, traveled a long time in the forest before daylight, then hid again. Even though the rest of the Osage were still after him, he got completely away to thong more trail marker trees."

"What do you mean, 'the rest of the Osage,' Grandpa? Who was missing?".

"Well, Tyler," said Grandpa, looking over at his wife. "I guess you're old enough to hear it all." Grandpa grunted slightly and shifted his leg to ease the pain in his foot.

"On top of the bluff the young scout was jumped by one of the Osage who had been sent to watch. There was some sort of fracas—it was in the dark, you know. Runs-to-Earth killed the other fellow, stabbed him with his knife. Course that really made the other Indians madder when they found the warrior's body later. The Cherokee had outwitted the bunch . . . and outfought one of them."

"Geeeeeee," Tyler exclaimed in a low voice. "He killed him. Wow!"

"Richard," Grandma said rather sharply to Grandpa, "maybe you shouldn't have told Tyler tonight. He might not sleep too well, especially after all his adventures."

"Oh, Helen, he'll be just fine. He grew up a lot today."

As the truck bounced its way down the steep, rutted logging road, Tyler looked into the dark woods, remembering and thinking. Firmly fixed now in his heart was Runs-to-Earth, the Cherokee trail marker. His ancestor. And he was glad.

Historical Note

This story is based loosely on fact. The two thong trees and the dog Rachel actually exist in the St. Francis River Valley of rural Madison County, Missouri.

The hickory grows in the middle of much younger trees. Its estimated age is 170 years. The huge oak is deep in a ravine on the north slope of a forested hill. It does not, as the oak in the story did, point to a river crossing. When this area was logged seventy to eighty years ago, these two trees were spared because their ninety-degree bends and numerous knots made them unsuitable for wood products.

"Message" or thong trees were used widely by Indian tribes, particularly those who lived in forested areas. Many kinds of hardwood trees scattered throughout the United States from the East Coast to the Rocky Mountains were bent. Quite a few still stand, especially in the eastern part of the country.

The only way to be reasonably sure any strange, bent tree in the woods was made by Indian hands and not by natural forces, such as falling trees, winds, storms, and the like, is to look for signs of pressure damage—

thong scars—in the bark under the first bend and on top of the second.

Today, no one knows exactly how to read these ancient trees. It is doubtful if earlier settlers did either. Sometimes the messages signified more than just the directions in which the trees point. The Indians also caused knobs or other scarifying marks to grow on the bent trees. These marks added all kinds of other information such as "Don't go any further," or "Entering hostile country."

The Indians in this story could have lived at any time from 1785 through 1839, though the earlier time is more likely. As early as 1785 a few Cherokee were in the St. Francis River Valley. Some of the physically imposing and powerful Osage were still living in portions of eastern Missouri at that time. After the Louisiana Purchase in 1803, and under increasing pressure from the U.S. government, families of Shawnee, Delaware, Sac, Miami, Choctaw, Creek, Chickasaw, and additional Cherokee had left their lands and moved into the new territory in what is now the southeastern portion of Missouri.

In the early 1800s the Osage were located in western Missouri territory. And by 1830, due to land cessions they made to the U.S. around 1808, 1818, and 1825, the Osage had been relocated to reservation life in what is now modern Kansas and Oklahoma. However, their men continued to go out on war parties and hunting expeditions to all surrounding lands. This tribe was noted (among all American Indian tribes) for the size of its people, warriors often being more than six feet in height. One of their more famous chiefs, Shonkah Sabe, was seven feet tall and weighed 250 pounds.

During the years 1838–39, the United States government removed most of the Cherokee Indians from their ancestral mountain homes in North Carolina, Tennessee, and Georgia to prairie land that is now Oklahoma. So many died—some authorities claim as many as 4,000—the Cherokee call this long march the "Trail of Tears."

There were two primary trails. One proceeded through northern Arkansas, the other through southern Missouri. The St. Francis River lay directly in the path of the second trail. Some individuals and a few families of Cherokee managed to flee the march and hide in the hills, which were so like those of their beloved homelands.

Bibliography

Chapman, Carl H. and Eleanor F. INDIANS AND ARCHEOLOGY OF MISSOURI, rev. ed. University of Missouri Press, Columbia, MO, 1983.

Fleming, Paula Richardson and Judith Luskey. THE NORTH AMERICAN INDIANS. Harper & Row, New York, 1986.

Gilbert, Joan. "Walking the Trail of Tears," RURAL MISSOURI MAGAZINE, April, 1985.

Hothem, Lar. NORTH AMERICAN INDIAN ARTI-FACTS, 3rd ed. (Collectors Identification and Value Guide Series). Books Americana, Florence, AL, 1984.

Hunt, W. Ben. THE COMPLETE HOW-TO BOOK OF INDIAN CRAFT. Macmillan, New York, 1973.

Ingenthron, Elmo. INDIANS OF THE OZARK PLA-TEAU. The School of the Ozarks Press, Springfield, MO, 1970.

LaFarge, Oliver. A PICTORIAL HISTORY OF THE NORTH AMERICAN INDIAN. Crown Publishers, New York, 1956.

Maddux, Teresa. "Timber Talk," MISSOURI CONSERVATION MAGAZINE. no date.

Orchard, William C. BEADS AND BEADWORK OF THE AMERICAN INDIANS, 2nd ed. Museum of the American Indian, New York, 1975.

Rhodes, Richard. THE OZARKS. Time-Life Books, New York, 1974.

Underwood, Thomas B. STORY OF THE CHEROKEE PEOPLE. Cherokee Publications, Cherokee, NC, 1961.

Utley, Robert M. and Wilcomb E. Washburn. THE INDIAN WARS (American Heritage Library). Houghton Mifflin, New York, 1985.

Waldman, Carl. ATLAS OF THE NORTH AMERICAN INDIAN. Facts on File Publications, New York, 1985.

White, George M. CRAFT MANUAL OF NORTH AMERICAN INDIAN FOOTWEAR. Self-Published, Ronan, MT, 1969.

Wilkins, Thurman. CHEROKEE TRAGEDY: The Story of the Ridge Family and the Decimation of a People. Macmillan, New York, 1970.

Wilson, Terry P. THE OSAGE (Indians of North America Series). Chelsea House, New York, 1988.